Find
Anthony
Ant

First American edition published in 2006
by Boxer Books Limited.

Distributed in the United States and Canada by
Sterling Publishing Co., Inc.
387 Park Avenue South, New York, NY 10016-8810

First published in Great Britain in 2006
by Boxer Books Limited.
www.boxerbooks.com

First published in the United States and Canada in 1993
by Random House Children's Books,
under the title *Amazing Anthony Ant*.

Text copyright © 1993 Lorna Philpot
Illustrations copyright © 1993 Graham Philpot

The rights of Lorna and Graham Philpot to be identified as the author
and illustrator of this work have been asserted by them
in accordance with the Copyright, Designs and Patents Act, 1988.

All rights reserved, including the right of reproduction in whole or in part in any form.
Library of Congress Cataloging-in-Publication Data available.

ISBN 10: 1-905417-10-1
ISBN 13: 978-1-905417-10-0

Printed in China

For Ann,
David, and Nicola

Are you an amazing
Anthony Ant finder?
If so, can you find the Anthony Ant
that is different from the others
on the endpapers
of this book?

Find Anthony Ant

Lorna and Graham Philpot

Start here

THE ANTHONY ANT WAY IN

THE ANTHONY ANT WAY OUT

Boxer Books

1

The ants came marching **one by one.** Anthony stopped...

BEETLE LANE

PLUM TREE TRUNK ROAD

Grub Shop

 or  or

To eat
a plum?

To buy
bubble gum?

To beat
a drum?

Find Anthony Ant.

APHID ALLEY

The Beetles
in Concert

2

The ants came marching
two by two.
Anthony stopped...

ONION SPRINGS

ANT HILL BROOK

ANT COLONY MARSHES

PLAYunderGROUND

   or      or

To tie   To cry   To look
his shoe?   boo-hoo?   for a clue?

Find Anthony Ant.

GALLERY ALLEY

Ant Gallery

GALLERY GROVE

3

The ants came marching
three by three.
Anthony stopped...

 or  or

To climb
a tree?

To watch
TV?

Because he
hurt his knee?

Find Anthony Ant.

ANTISEPTIC STREET

Doctor Ant

SKULL AND CROSSBONE ROAD

4

The ants came marching
four by four.
Anthony stopped…

 or  or

To knock on
the door?

To ask
for more?

To sweep
the floor?

Find Anthony Ant.

ANTHRACITE VALE

Oliver's Restaur'ant

WEEVIL WAY

WORKER ANT WALK

5

The ants came marching
five by five.
Anthony stopped...

 or  or

To visit
a hive?

To jiggle
and jive?

To go for
a drive?

Find Anthony Ant.

Venus Ant trap

Underground RAVE

SPRING ROAD

Sub Aqua Ant

WORM HOLE WELL

6

The ants came marching
six by six.
Anthony stopped…

EARTHWORM WAY

ROTTEN ROW ROUTE

PLANTATION PLACE

Ant Nursery

 or  or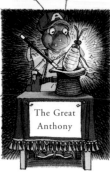

To tickle
the chicks?

To stack
the bricks?

To perform
magic tricks?

Find Anthony Ant.

ROTTEN WOOD WAY

BEECH TREE ROUTE

ANT-THEATRE

1

2

3

7

The ants came marching
seven by seven.
Anthony stopped...

 or  or

To chat with Kevin?   To hide in a cavern?   To count to eleven?

Find Anthony Ant.

8

The ants came marching
eight by eight.
Anthony stopped...

FRAGRANT GARDENS

RED COLONY CASTLE

BATTLEMENT

 or  or

To lick his plate? To look for a gate? To check his weight?

Find Anthony Ant.

MAIN DRAIN STREET

WALK

9

The ants came marching

nine by nine.

Anthony stopped...

APPLE CORE COURT

UNDERWEAR WAY

Ants in Pants

APPLE TREE ROUTE

 or  or

To hang socks on the line?   To read a sign?   To shout, "That hat's mine"?

Find Anthony Ant.

FAIRY RING ROAD

DIAMOND RING ROAD

10

The ants came marching
ten by ten.
Anthony stopped...

 or  or

To feed the hen? To write with a pen? To read it again?

Find Anthony Ant.

Way In

Way Out

ALL ANTS' WAY

SKELETON · EAST · END

Did you find me?